My Shadow

By Dharma Eyer

Published by *LIBERTY UNDER ATTACK PUBLICATIONS*, July 2020

ISBN: 9798657399905

Publisher Information:
Website: www.libertyunderattack.com
Contact: shane@libertyunderattack.com

Interior Design By: Shane Radliff

<u>Acknowledgements</u>

I've been fortunate to have many cheerleaders in my life to have encouraged me to keep going. Specifically, I'd like to thank Tony, Ernest, Amber, Zack, Nick, Rachel/Megan/Shane, Berlin, & LUA Publications. Big thanks to the community, you inspire me.

<u>Dedication:</u>

Dedicated to the shadow that lives within us all.

Foreword

Introduction

I hide from my shadow self. She is scary...lurking inside. A seemingly harmless child. She is ordinary in every way, by looks alone. Golden hair pulled into pigtails, sapphire eyes, creamy skin. But when she opens her mouth, locusts and moths fly from it.

Screams in every octave escape her lips. Tortured souls gasp and gurgle longing for escape.

There is no peace with her. No calm. She is a storm. An impending doom.

Despite being smaller than average, the earth shakes from her mighty step, the weight in her feet allowing others to feel her journey. Her need to suffer, her will to endure the torture. When the wind blows, it seems to whisper her name. Calling to her for help; the wind knows it doesn't want to go to some places, but only she has the courage to lead.

The sun lights her way in the growing darkness. Helping her out of fear from being put out, like a flame.

Her touch is ice cold, absent of warmth in every way. Her eyes are hollow, only a fragment of what used to live inside. The embers that burn within her now only consume life, leaving remnants of the girl she was. In her own heart lives the darkest of shadows. A place so absent of light, not even the brightest of lights will venture. A black hole, consuming, feeding the darkness.

The walls of her heart still echo her pleas to turn her darker still. Her skin muddied with bruises and sticky with saliva from protectors gone rogue. Her mouth tastes like their blood, her tongue swollen from the bites and nibbles, her fingers raw from digging, her wrists bloodied from the binds, her knees scuffed and cut from the begging. Her inner thighs streaked, stained and scratched. Her cheeks left with a graveyard of tears shed. Lines tracing down her pale cheeks.

She walks alone, free from the warmth of others. She is lost but knows exactly where she is going.

The darkness inside her belly can never be satiated.

Part One

I hate the wind

I hate the mind

Wind and mind

The wind blows like mind

Tossing ideas around

Swirling the calm as water circles a drain

The mind seems to scramble the truth

Distorting the real

Everything is caught up in the chaos

Anxiety responds like leaves adrift a gust of mind

Chapter One

The car horns are my least favorite part of the city. No one is moving, what good is it to honk? I am so tired of the noise, in general. The panhandlers, the busses, the people. I'm *so sick* of the people. More interested in digital relationships over real ones. More interested in selfies and talking about dumb things that didn't matter, like what celebrity was locked in what spicy scandal. Mostly though, I'm tired of feeling incomplete. I'll be 40 in a few years, and what do I have to show for it? An empty apartment, a successful, but peaked, career, dining alone on take out. My life, on paper, is an 'insert-successful-life-here', except that life does not seem to be mine, it feels like I'm only the placeholder.

I feel so confused all the time. I feel all alone; that sinking feeling of emptiness is ever-present, deep in my gut. Like I've lost something belonging to me; shit, I can't even describe what I've lost. I feel like a piece of me was left, on a path, to remind me what route I took to get home, except I took a different way back, leaving my marker there. This feeling made me bitter and angry and living in a big city seemed to exacerbate things. I used to be popular, I guess; I had a lot of options in casual friends to hang out with. We'd go to movies, out to dinner, dancing: typical young, single stuff. I've always cherished my alone time, but I never had to be alone; I could call anyone at any time and have a blast. As I've aged, however, I've lost friends to marriage or children, or just lost 'em. I've always been a loner, but now, I wasn't alone by choice. Being alone seems harder these days. The sun colder, the dark, bleaker. The years passed and I left my apartment less and less. Until now, I leave for work only. I have my meals delivered, groceries delivered, I even have a housekeeper. I have no need to ever leave anymore. Other than this damn job.

To pass the time on earth, I recently picked up reading. Magazines mostly. I bought thirty magazine subscriptions over the past few months. Every topic you can imagine. My mail carrier hates me; I don't care. I read about two to three magazines, cover-to-cover, a night. I don't have television, nor would I watch anyway, too much noise. So, I sit, and I read.

I used to enjoy going out for pleasure. There are few things that bring me more joy than to have a picnic or go camping. But anymore, I come home from work with more anxiety than what I left with. It's so defeating to try and muster the energy to cope with the feelings. The rage, mostly. But the hurt seemed to be magnified by the loneliness; and as a result, I try to tune out the loneliness any way that I can. Listening to music, reading, and smoking the occasional joint seems to tune things out fine enough.

Four new magazines arrived today, I'm eager to read them. One that I'm especially looking forward to reading is a high gloss, slick-paged movie-making magazine. All about movie ins-and-outs like lighting, directing, tips and tricks, full of vibrant color photos. Each has the rich, saturated ink smell that licks at my face as I flip through the pages. As I'm perusing the pages and topics, I come across a peculiar page. The page in question has a random image in the middle. Not fancy or ornate, just the opposite. The picture is of a faded color print, an in-bloom purple anemone stem. The color on the image, though faded in comparison by the rest of the magazine, is more a natural ink. The smell of the page is different. My eyes are drawn all over the matte paper. The background of the paper is that dark white, not white, not blue, not brown, or gray...somewhere in between. It's that classic recycled, thick textured, homemade paper look. The page has the feel of an old t-shirt, soft and warm. It really compliments the crisp flower image.

The page is so much different than the others, though it's the same size as the neighboring pages. I stare at the image for what seems like an hour. Looking over every single inch of the page. Curious, I look for the origin of the page. Is it an advertisement, a different piece of mail stuffed in the pages in error? In my surprise, I find a thread, peeking up through the top of the binding. The page has been stitched in...how odd. Magazines are not stitched, they are glued, yet this page seems to have been hand-stitched near the middle of the magazine. I cannot see the stitching from the binding exterior. The stitching is only to the inner pages, as if it was stitched in and then glued together. Obviously, on purpose. A single stem with a lovely purple flower filling the middle of the page, leaving nothing but blankness in a border all around.

The flower seems familiar. It sparks a memory. I knew a girl back when I was 19 and living on the street.

Man, that was a long time ago...what was her name?

I can't remember. I seem to recall she was the youngest I met, maybe 15? She had this exact picture of the flower tattooed on her leg. It was beautiful work.

God, what was her name?

I look at the picture again. Funny, to think of her after all this time. I have not thought of those days in a long while.

I feel pressure start to build around my head. My eyes are feeling "full", so I take a break from studying the image. I feel exhausted and make the decision to circumvent the headache and lay down for a bit. I put the peculiar ad and magazine on the floor with the image up, next to me, and I stretch out on the couch. It's not long before I drift off to sleep and begin to dream...

I awake in the dark hotel room; I have no idea what time or day it is. I routinely feel for my old journal in its usual place underneath my pillow. Heather is on the floor in her standard sleeping pose. I hate it here. The musty smell, the television with no channels. Heather is weird. I don't trust her...something about her seems...off. Heather is a thin, young girl. Blonde, pixie cut, freckles, glossy blue eyes. A pretty girl. Though she is younger than me, she's been homeless far longer. It shows. She is cagey, distrusting, and violent. She sleeps in a pile under the desk of the hotel, every night. Only one leg sticks out from under the table. A short, tan, and dirty leg, with a beautiful tattoo on her calf of a stem attached to a perfectly in-bloom purple anemone flower. What's-His-Face said she is too young to get the tat in a shop, so some friend she was blowing for a place to sleep did the work. He says she finds herself in men's' beds a lot, but since I've known her, she's only ever slept under the desk. I don't trust him either. His beady little eyes, he gives me the creeps, but luckily, he seems only interested in Heather. In the three weeks that I've been with Heather and What's-His-Name, I've had to fight almost weekly. This has been the hardest few weeks since I've been homeless the past two years. I don't stay with the same group of Broken Puppets for long. If people only knew how many Broken Puppets there are in the world, they'd flip. A year ago, I came up with the name, Broken Puppets for them all. Seemed pretty fitting, children mostly. Abused, neglected, thrown away, forgotten. Heather's a Broken Puppet, I guess so am I. Heather and I have a lot in common, despite being so different. Heather's story was her mom's new husband really loved Heather a lot. When her mom got a job working nights, her new parental figure began fucking her every night while her mom was away. Heather worked up the courage, one night after a few weeks of regular abuse, and told her mom. As a result, her mom kicked her out. Heather said that the last thing her mom ever said to her was, "No whores allowed". That was a few years ago, now. I never told, I just left. I guess sometimes, you're damned if you do, and damned if you don't. Folks would be surprised though. Heather, me, What's-His-Name... we're just a couple among millions. I've traveled with about twenty different groups of Broken Puppets. Kids that ran away from Kid-Fuckers, kids that ran away from druggie parents, kids like Heather....Although, Heather might have been the luckiest of all the kids I'd met. We're all broken; once your doll loses an eye, she doesn't get played with anymore. Just like the doll, we're just tossed away like garbage. We all have one thing in common, trauma. Trauma has united us. It made us a misfit army. Most all have fallen into a clique or a group that they travel and eat with, but not me. I trust no one, I don't let anyone in, but I need places to stay and sometimes I must assimilate to eat. But I never stay long. The risk of danger is too great in one place, with one group. I must keep moving...but not right now. I reach up and feel my familiar journal again, touching its cover and binding. I pull my hand back from under the pillow, rub my eyes, and yawn a gaping mouth and lungs full of oxygen. 'Later', I think, I roll over on the stinky mattress, trying to stop thinking of my hopelessness, the hunger pangs. I quickly drift off back asleep.

I awake on the couch, in my Uptown city loft. The back of my neck and the couch are wet. I hate dreaming of *them*. It makes me cry, every time. Pretty happy the headache did not come along, though. I find the magazine flipped to the dull, old t-shirt page with the picture of the purple anemone on it. It occurs to me, looking at it with fresh eyes, that there are no words, a website, or a phone number. The method to advertise here was intriguing. Whoever spent the money on this ad is in big trouble since there is no website.

I move on to the next magazine.

Chapter Two

The last few weeks have been busy at work. Pulling close to sixty hours per week and I've have had little time to read, recreationally. My stack of magazines is now about thirty deep. Piling up the stack of slick pages, it often topples over, pissing my housekeeper off. Hopefully I can read a few tonight.

Looking forward to a quiet evening at home, I plan out my reading itinerary, first I'll read my new health magazine, then, my new Rolling Stone...who knows after that. I slowly walk up the three flights of stairs, noticing the weight in my legs as I pull them up. I decide to dial my favorite take out place and order dinner before I get too high. Hopefully it's early enough, and the driver will have time to deliver before I'm forced to eat the old olives in my fridge. I get my door unlocked and toss my keys in the side table bowl. I shed my coat and laptop bag on the floor directly in front of the front door, completely ignoring the expensive coat rack that I *had to have* the previous year. I find my spot in the couch, the one with the familiar slump in the cushion where I sit every night. I shuffle through the teetering pile of reading and find the Rolling Stone, "Change of plans, you first!" I tell the slick pages. I love the feel of the glossy finish, smooth and cold under my fingers. I take in the cover, looking at the band, the highlights of what treasures are contained within these colorful pages. I take in the smell of the ink from the printing and fan the pages from the front to the back, letting the breeze tickle my eye lashes, smelling the earthy metallic smell of the ink.

Amazingly...I see the same advertisement of the purple anemone on the same kind of paper and again stitched to the center of a rock-and roll-periodical. This has produced a sick feeling in my tummy and ushered in a sour bile taste in my mouth. It was almost like the flower is meant for me, and only me. It sings to me, as the memories flood in from my past. The crushing feeling of loneliness raises the hair on my arms. "You're overreacting. It's just a picture of a flower. Someone fucked up, spent a bunch of money on this ad and did not proof it; now, it's too late and the advertiser was snubbed. I see it all the time in my work..." I lied to myself. I mean, sure that is possible, and it does happen a lot; however, this felt different. This felt like I was being targeted. *Who else knows this image?* This exact image of the flower. I guess Heather and whoever rolled with her, but...who knows if they are even alive anymore. That was years ago.

No, this flower feels personal to me.

In order to get past the bile taste, I decide to move on to a different magazine. I flip through the pages of the health magazine, but I'm clearly distracted. I notice nothing contained within the pages and decide I'm done reading for a while and go for a walk.

I'm already three blocks from home before I realize that I'm on a walk. Something that I have not done in years. The shock that I am out and actually enjoying myself is enough to keep me distracted. I walk to my favorite haunts, before I became a shut-in. A little Mexican bakery, the Panadaria had the best sweet rolls. I forgot how the smell of the baking treats would call to me like sirens on a rocky shore. I went to the harbor next, and finished the evening by watching the sunset and the boats pull into the docks. I'm suddenly startled and pulled away from my peace when my phone rings. It's a number I don't recognize. I let the voicemail catch it. The text that follows, reads, "Hey, Its Jade Dragon. I'm here with your order".

It's my dinner. Shit.

Chapter Three

Saturday morning, I wake up with a headache again. They're becoming more frequent. I had wanted to pop into the office today to get a few extra things done to ready myself for Monday; however, I really need to get some reading done so that I can throw away some of these magazines. I boil some water for my coffee and decide I'll organize my reading itinerary while the coffee brews.

When the kettle screams, I pour the water over the grounds in my French press and set my oven timer. Then, the difficult task of choosing which one I'll read when I drink coffee and which one I'll read when I eat breakfast later. *I'll make quick work of this reading in no time*, I encourage. I find my biggest coffee mug and I pour the freshly made coffee, count out five sugar spoons of sugar, stir with a random spoon I found on my counter, and walk with determination to the couch.

I pick up the first magazine. It's one on alternative lifestyles. The colors are all mostly rainbows and pastels, the pages are just as slick and high gloss as the other expensive magazines in the pile. In regular fashion, I fan the pages out letting the breeze kiss my face, and again...there, nestled among the center pages, is the advertisement of the flower. *Am I in space?* Three very different magazines with the same ad, which was extremely strange from an advertising perspective. Usually a company had a "target" audience and they designed specific ads for that particular demographic. But three very different audiences and the exact same ad...Very unconventional.

Curious, I reach for the two other two subscriptions that enclosed the flower advertisement and I compare all three images. All are eerily the same: same style of paper, but in handmade fashion, each with a unique mix of speckles and patterns of the flecks of color used to produce the page. The stitching on all three had the same thread, however, each thread seemingly unique as if it were handspun thread. The thin twist on all three were each twisted in different tautness.

The image, however, on all three was identical. Not a single shadow or glisten of dew was out of place. I am struck with awe by the time and the sheer cost, and am a little offended that the ad company missed the website or other identifying marker...Anything.

My mind ducks out a side door and I remember *her* again, Heather. I had traveled with many groups during those days. All mostly kids, some adults and old folks, too. We were the nomadic tribes of street rats. Stopping under pre-arranged, commonly known bridges, overpasses, and parks with extra overgrowth. Anywhere kids could go and seemingly disappear from a society that treated them as an inconvenience, a disease. True to a feral cat mentality, there was a lot of fighting and a lot of extra suffering.

The streets were dangerous. I made the decision to move on from Heather and the guy after the night I had to break the wine bottle over some other guy's head. After Heather, I tried to stay alone. It was risky to be a girl and on her own in the street, but I had so many trust issues, and it was also risky to be with others. Others brought risk, bad decisions, and an amount of hedonism that should have been outlawed. I mostly slept in construction sites of high-rise buildings. I'd have to wake up just before dawn to get moving in order to not get caught, but the skeletal buildings provided excellent weather cover and privacy. Having to wake early was a fair price. Consequently, however, I was constantly on the move.

I momentarily break from the memories and I glance down at my stomach...I sure was more fit then, I notice. A chill slides its way up my spine, and then I remember him....

Chapter Four

Shit! I overslept! I heard the talking first. In a panic, I throw my journal into my bag and I hurriedly roll up my sleeping bag and stuff it into my backpack. I scramble looking for an incomplete stairwell or a plastic-wrapped void in the drywall for a window, an exit. I slip out just as two overweight men wearing bright yellow hard hats enter the room. The plastic is still moving when they get through the framed-out threshold. I hop down to the ground and sprint for the fence. This has been my favorite place to sleep, I cannot get caught and fuck that up. I run until my lungs feel like they are going to pop in the cold air. I stop on a normally busy corner, but this time of morning, it's vacant. Strange to be here without the hordes of people shoving and shouting. After I catch my breath, I raise my arms to my head in order to ease an approaching side cramp. Lord, I hate waking up this way. I am so tired and all I can feel is my stomach being ripped apart, partly from the cramping but mostly from the hunger pains. "Jeez, when the hell I feed you last, tummy?" I say aloud. I can't recall my last meal. Two days ago? No, that was three days now, today. I decide this is as good of a place as any to panhandle for a few cents to buy a loaf of bread. I liked buying bread. It filled me quickly, twenty slices came in a sleeve and it was cheap. Mostly though, I didn't have to be on the street for long, begging for change. I don't like being exposed. I can feel myself start to change but I don't understand how just yet. I sit on the corner and wait for the sun. The night air is cold and I notice that I left my coat at the construction site…fuck. I decide to stand and just start walking to keep warm and hopefully by the time the sun makes his appearance I'll have found myself on a new busy street. As I walk, I consider using my sleeping bag to cover with, but decide against it. I don't like being exposed. There is something very noticeable about a person walking around at whatever the hell time this was in the morning adorned with a sleeping bag. So, I pick up the pace and keep walking.

By the time the sun finally lights my path, I notice that I am near a prison. I see the Don't Pick Up Hitcher sign, that is just my fucking luck. There is a busy road ahead that connects the prison road with the busy intersection a mile down, so I decided I will stop there and attempt to score a few bucks before finding a bodega for bread. I find a nice spot on a bench at a bus stop near the intersection. This is as good a place as any. I plop down, remove my bag and realize that it feels so good to just sit. The sun begins to warm my shoulders and I notice how beautiful the sunrise is today. The flies buzzing around a dumpster look like jewels. Their wings catch the sun in an iridescent shimmer, sparkling against the empty backdrop of the peaceful street without the mad dash of commuters. Small birds chase each other flirtingly, surely preparing for spring. The clouds and the sun paint together in the mornings, today was especially vivid with color. The splash of oranges, pinks, and the blues, purples caressed by the yellows and greens. The sky and the clouds share the color as if a brush is being dragged across a loaded pallet. It's stunning. I am totally engrossed in the beauty as the perfection fades away like the brush swirled in water, when I hear, "This seat taken?"

Startled, I jump over and like a stray cat, notice a well-dressed, kind-looking, young guy, not my age, older but younger. Maybe 21? He has a military style haircut and is wearing a military-looking uniform. "I wasn't fucking doing anything!" I snap defensively.

His eyes got big in response and his smile relaxed, "Whoa, sorry hon, I didn't mean to scare you, may I sit?"

"It's a free fucking country" I scoot farther to the side, smashing my ribs painfully into the side of the bench, debating whether or not to just get up. He sits far on the other side of the bench and I don't relax, though I am grateful for the space he leaves between us. He stares, face forward, and does not seem to move much. I can feel my back muscles start to relax though my heart is not convinced. My ribs call out in pain to move just shy of the armrest of the bench; however, I refuse. Another ten minutes pass, and my body relaxes enough to pull the bench from my sides. I take a big breath, more loudly than I would have liked from the pressure being removed. The guy turns his head and smiles a kind smile. I try not to look, other than out my peripheral view. I try and appear normal though it

occurs to me, I am not sure what that looks like exactly. I can feel my hands fidget and I start to wonder what the hell he wants. He tugs at his uniform jacket and chuckles to himself but loud enough for me to hear.

"Boy, I'm hungry. I guess I forgot breakfast. Have you eaten?" He turned his head and his smile was kind and big. The mention of hungry made my tummy growl loudly in response. My cheeks flash with hotness and his smile gets bigger. "Honey, you're just a little thing, you need to eat."

It's true, the past couple of years, I lost more weight than I had available. Standing just over five feet tall, I now probably weigh 85 pounds based on how my clothing fit. I think a couple of years ago they told me I was 110 pounds. There is no way I'm that big now. Before I can argue about not wanting food, he stands up and holds his hand in front of me as if he wants a dollar. I sit back and look at him.

He says, "C'mon, take my hand, you're going to be my breakfast date this morning." I stare at his hand for a good long while, and bless his heart, he stands there still holding his hand outstretched, looking like an idiot. Not moving. Finally, after assessing his uniform and his face, I stand up, ignoring his outstretched arm. Seemingly offended, he grunts and says, "Okay, Ms. Independent, I like it" chuckles, and walks along side of me. He gestures ahead to a greasy diner that smells like eggs and bacon as we approach. For a second, I think maybe just these smells would be enough to quell my hunger. My feet don't stop moving, though, and as he ushers me through the front door, I happily stride in. A feeling of euphoria washes over me: just the thought of eating in two, no, three days!

We sat at a booth in the corner of the room. I sat awkwardly, fidgeting over an upside-down coffee mug on the table. I kept my eyes on my hands. Not speaking. I couldn't even open the menu. I was afraid of being tempted by food that I had no money for. All I brought was an appetite. God what am I doing here?

The man ordered, but I paid no attention to what he asked for. After the waitress left our table, the man spoke, "Chad's my name. I work at the prison over there…. You and I look to be about the same age, how'd such a pretty girl get stuck on the streets? Ah shit, that's none of my business, you don't even know me, after all. Anyway, I ordered us a little something. You look like you haven't eaten in a week!"

"Three days." I replied.

"What?" he said.

"It's been three days since I'd eaten. I've gone longer, you know, its fine." I said, while keeping my eyes on my hands.

"You're a tough woman. I like that." He pushed the last part out of smiling lips.

I did not look, but one can tell when someone says something through a frown or a smile. I had never been called a woman before. It caught me off guard. My gaze stayed on my hands until the food came. I'm so afraid to look at the food. Chad, sitting politely, waiting to dig in, clears his throat, "Ahem…So…Ladies first?"

The smells are dancing around my head like a ribbon of warm baked biscuits, brown butter eggs, and salty, smoky bacon. My eyes tear up from the anticipation of being fed such a decadent meal after so many days of not eating. My stomach turns in disgust. I can feel the sick feeling rise in my stomach up to my esophagus. I'm so hungry, but the rich smells are so much. I'd been surviving on a loaf of bread per week and this was on another level. I sat waiting for the nausea to subside. I think maybe I can convince my tummy to take a piece of biscuit. My eyes slowly rise from my cracked finger tips to the plentiful plates of food. A pile of bacon bigger than I'd ever seen, it looked as if there were five pounds of thick cut, glistening marbled bacon. A basket full of the most fluffy biscuits that looked perfectly golden and crisp on the outside. As I imagine their internal secret fluffiness, the feelings of hunger begin to gain ground on the nausea. The eggs are fried in brown butter, with oozy, runny, golden middles. I'd never seen such a delightful spread.

"Please, I can see you're hungry, please take something. I bought more than enough for both of us." I feel my cheeks get hotter as my eyes well up with burning liquid. I bow my head and squeeze my eyes shut, the tears roll to the apple of my cheeks before dropping to my lap. "Thank you," I say quietly to no one in particular. I look up and see Chad looking at me. He is smiling a kind smile, still waiting for me to make the first move toward the generous bounty. I slowly reach for a biscuit, my mouth watering so much I feel like I have to swallow spit to keep from drooling. At this rate, I'll be full of spit before I even get a piece of biscuit in my mouth. I push both my thumbs into the side of the biscuit and feel a familiar crack in the perfectly crispy outside crust; my fingers sink into the soft and warm middle, breaking apart and revealing a cloud like center. My eyes begin to well up again at the sheer beauty of the biscuit. I peel the biscuit all the way apart and remove a center piece of the cloud and bring the steaming bread to my lips. I stuff the piece deep in my mouth so it couldn't accidentally fall out. The biscuit is everything I'd hoped it would be. My tummy growls a thunderous rumble as if to say, MORE! Chad watches me enjoy the biscuit before he happily grabs handful-after-handful of food from each plate and begins to hurriedly shovel the food into his mouth. I think about the eggs and the bacon, but I am not sure I'd be able to keep it down. I think best to just work on the biscuit. After the first biscuit went down, the thought of eating other morsels seemed more feasible.

True to fashion, I was becoming the feral cat that I noticed in the other broken puppets. Chad and I met for breakfast a few times a week for some time. I kept coming back because it was an easy meal. I minded less and less as I got to know Chad. We seemed to understand each other pretty well. It was nice to have a friendship. I guess I consider it a friendship because he feeds me and that's the sort of thing I always imagined that friends do with each other. On the second consecutive month of meeting Chad at the familiar bench near the prison, he asked me to move in with him.

"No funny business! I have a spare bedroom. I own my house, no rent. Whatcha say, Kid? It might help you get back on your feet."

It seemed like an easy yes. I practically knew Chad after eating with him for so long and how nice would it be to have a bed again? I gave it a quick thought and happily nodded in agreement. After breakfast, we moved pretty quickly. As we walked out of the restaurant, he asked if I had other stuff somewhere that needed to be grabbed. I explained that I only had this backpack, showing him the old backpack that secured a sleeping bag and a journal that I wrote in sometimes. I appreciated his quick action; it will be nice to make myself at home. I climbed into his massive, black truck and we headed to his little green house at the edge of town. It was nicer than what I imagined. Then again, I was not sure what I imagined. The home was a mint green with white shutters. It was a one-story with a chain link fence around a small yard, and a pine tree in the corner of the lot. The front door was white with a heart-shaped cut out window in the front middle.

Chad was so young to own his home. He was only a few years older than me. These people that seemed good at life, I secretly hated them for how easy they made it seem. Chad hopped out of his truck and walked to my side, opening the door for me. I grabbed my backpack and took his extended hand to help me climb down from the truck cabin. I throw the backpack over my right shoulder and I follow closely behind him, excited for what lies on the other side of the sweetheart, cutout door. He unlocks the door, holds it open for me, and motions for me to walk in. Aesthetically, the inside resembles the '70s: brown shag carpet, wood paneled walls. Though it's dated, it's clean and the beds are neatly made as if no one had slept in either one, ever. It was all so perfect. I excitedly called, "Which room is mine?" Silence. I paid no mind to his lack of answer, deciding I would pop around and have a look at the rest of the house.

As I begin my journey down a hall, Chad, seemingly out of nowhere, grabs my arm with firm determination and barks, "Where are YOU going?"

Startled, I whimper and wince in pain and surprise, but try and shrug it off, chuckling nervously, "Oh stop, I am just checking out your home is all." He lets go of my arm but doesn't say anything, my arm immediately throbs where his fingers dug into my flesh. I notice crescent moon shapes in my bicep where his fingernails dug deeper than his already pressing finger tips. Startled, I rub my arm and decide against the unguided tour. Instead, I take a seat at the kitchen table for a while. I take off the backpack and hang it from the back of a chair and sit down. At least until my arm feels better.

He walks over to me and puts his hand on my shoulders, and very gently kisses me sweetly on the forehead, "I'm sorry, Kid. I have to go to work soon, I get a little on edge before working at the prison. I'm sure you can imagine. I'm sorry, it won't happen again."

I begin to relax and wonder how tough one must be to work in a prison full of dangerous thugs. I shrug off his outburst and look for the bathroom. When I return to the table, he is sitting in the opposite chair. He gets up and moves over his chair next to mine on the same side of the small table. It seemed curious as we were only previously a foot from each other. We'd sat farther apart at the diner. Yet, he moves closer still. He reaches his hand over to my thigh. I jump a bit, but he smiles a sweet smile and rubs my thigh slowly from the outside to the top. I am grateful for the place to stay and don't want my caginess to make trouble for my new arrangements; however, my skin begins to crawl. I stay put out of obligation as he begins to move his hand with moderate pressure slowly to my inner thigh, halfway from my knee to my groin area. I feel myself push back with my legs attempting to gain some ground between us but as I begin to move back, he moved his hand up to my throat, cutting off a good portion of my oxygen supply. While I attempt to gasp for air, he pulls my face close to his and kisses my lips before letting go, shoving me down, hard on my chair and getting up to leave for work. It was so abrupt and sudden, and the kiss startled me. I was not here for a romantic interest. He was my friend...wasn't he? Chad grabbed his hat and his keys and left for work without saying a word, without even looking in my direction. After he left, I heard the door lock and I relaxed a bit. My stomach still felt a little queasy, but I was okay. I grabbed my backpack and walked to the far, smaller bedroom and decided this one must be mine, since the room had nothing but a made bed and one closet inside. I sat down on the twin-size bed, taking out the journal and putting it under my pillow. Then, I proceeded to hang the backpack up in the closet. I had a closet. That was far out! I was tired and decided I would lay down in my new bed a while. I fell asleep almost immediately.

Chad had returned sometime while I was asleep, either late at night or early in the morning. It felt so good to sleep in a bed that I slept so soundly, never hearing him return home. The next morning, he was already awake, preparing breakfast... The combination of food/coffee smells were enticing. I happily awoke and we dined together like we had for the previous months at the diner. It was nice to have a little slice of normal. After breakfast, I offered to help with dishes and clean up, I really feeling like this was going to work. As I washed and he rinsed and dried, I noticed his eyes wander to my chest. I decided it was all in my head, that I was paranoid after his weird behavior. But to maybe stave off any possible interest, I say, "Boy, I have not had a shower in god knows how long. Would you mind if I bathed today?"

He did not reply.

After I had let the plug out of the sink to drain of the water, he reached over and grabbed a handful of my right butt cheek so hard I cried out in pain. He pulled my hips toward him by his claw of my flesh and whispered in my ear, "You are going to be very popular! Tight little ass." I fought to pull free and fell to the floor before his face erupted in roaring laughter. "Oh relax! I'm just fucking with ya. Jeez! Go ahead and wash your self after I leave for work. Towels are in the hall closet just outside the bathroom."

I found nothing about any of that funny. I decided I was not in a great place, but I just needed to make the best of it and maybe spend less time with Chad. My guard began to rise, and I was a little afraid that I was not supposed to be there. That I had made a mistake, but I tried to just relax. After he had left for work and I heard the familiar lock behind him, I found a towel and took the longest, hottest shower I could recall in years. It was amazing, I felt so relaxed and more like a person than ever. I made a sandwich and after washing my plate, decided I would go to bed. I had put a chair from the kitchen table against the door handle to wedge the door closed, just in case.

Again, Chad returned from work before morning. I stayed in my room most of the day the next day, writing the last few days' events in my journal. He knocked loudly mid-day demanding I come out and eat something. "Kid, where's the other kitchen chair? Is it in there? Are you okay? I don't think you've eaten in a while. C'mon on out, kid. I'm worried about you."

He sounded genuinely concerned that I had not come out or eaten since last night. I thought I had better at least give it a try. The bed was amazing to sleep in, I should probably avoid doing anything to jeopardize that. I stuffed the journal back under my pillow and emerged from the guest bedroom. He, again, had a beautiful breakfast prepared. Freshly squeezed orange juice, pancakes, bacon, and real maple syrup. The smells were enticing. We enjoyed our breakfast and kept the talking to a minimum.

After breakfast, I again began to help clean up when Chad grabbed me by the front of the waistband in my pants, holding me by the zipper with his other hand, pulling me close again and planting a hard kiss into my face before throwing me to the ground. He threw me with such force that I slid backward, hitting the wall head first. I was slouched-up against the wall like a rag doll, my body was stunned; however, my eyes were open and my mind was fully aware of what was happening. Dazed, I lay there, watching Chad pull up a chair in front of my lifeless body. He sits reverse on the chair with the back of the chair to his chest, "Here is how this is going to go. Nothing is free, you little whore. You work for me to earn that bed. I'm going to work, and when I get back, I have a whole shit load of clients that have booked you solid. You will earn that bed, but who knows when you'll be here to sleep in it." He laughed a loud and evil belly laugh, tilting his head to the sky; his wild eyes seemed to glow with fury. My body went cold as it started to wake up and join my mind. I heard a throat-y, nasal sucking, and before I realized what the noise was, I felt a warm, slimy ball of goopy spit hit me in my face. It slid from my forehead down to my cheek, dripping to the floor. Chad gets up, spins the chair back around to the table, and walks out, locking the front door behind him. I can finally move my arms, and so wipe the stringy mucus from my face trying hard to not throw up the bacon. The panic fills me up and I scramble to my feet. What the fuck have I done? I run to the front door, but I see immediately that it's a double deadbolt door, and I don't have the interior key to escape. I run wildly to each room; all the windows have been nailed shut from the outside. How did I not notice all of this when I first walked in here? I am trapped on the inside. I don't know how long he will be gone, nor who my clients were, and I did not intend on finding out. I considered breaking a window before I found the door to the garage unlocked. How fucking fortunate! I ran into the garage looking for the door opener. I try and pry the door open by hand, but I'm simply not strong enough. I see another possible exit next to the garage door and run over to it. The door is locked, but it's such an ill-fitting door that I only have to wiggle it up and down a few times before I'm able to work the lock free from the frame. The door swings open and I'm met with a cool breeze and hot sun. I run wildly toward town. I have no idea where I am going, but I just run, leaving behind my journal and my backpack.

I break from my flashback to throw up in the sink. Leaving that journal still haunts me to this day. I had that journal forever. I wrote everything I had ever endured into that journal. It had become my one and only prized possession. A sadness overtook my mind, accompanied by regret. I had never really considered what all I had endured at such an innocent age of 19. I had endured so much by that age. My head began to spin. It was as if I'd never considered what all I'd gone through in my lifetime. I guess it was something that one could not dwell on. In the words of NWA, you just gotta keep grinding.

It was because of that traumatic experience with Chad that I stayed alone, only remaining "friends" with people like Heather for short periods of time, keeping everyone else away; in other words, having no real personal relationships with anyone.

After being released from the hospital, I had locked Shadow up. It was her or me, and I thought it had to be me. I locked her away and lived on the streets with the broken puppets for years before relocating to the city three years later and defeating homelessness at the ripe age of twenty. It was in the city that I got my lucky break. I worked in restaurants for a few years before wandering inside a real estate office boasting my artistic skills, landing myself a job. I had worked my ass off from those humble beginnings to the advertising executive that I am today.

Damn, best not to think about this shit too much.

I decide that is enough reminiscing for a while. I skip the reading and just eat a quiet breakfast instead. *I think I'll get out of the house and see a matinee today.* It will be nice to get out of the house again; I had not gotten out since going for my walk.

I missed it, weirdly.

Chapter Five

The commute to work on Monday was a nightmare: the busses were late, as traffic was backed up for hours due to multiple accidents. It was a mess. Then again, the first day of sunlight in months and it makes everyone go crazy. Standing, waiting for the bus, I happen to notice a teenager presumably on her way to school. She was ordinary, dressed in black, tight pants, a black hoodie, black, dyed hair, paired with blonde eyebrows. Her face was painted in angst with dark circles under such young eyes. What made me perk up to this child, however, was the pinned advertisement of the flower to her backpack in true punk fashion. The safety pins carefully placed so as to not to tear the delicate handmade paper. It almost seemed to unravel the knot in my stomach. I think and lie to myself, "See, the ad was not meant for me in some weird universal message." But seeing the image and thinking of my past seemed to oddly give me peace despite the memories being anything but peaceful. The bus finally arrived and I moved to the back of the bus, where I happened to see an older woman, dressed as a cleaning lady with the eerie advertisement, trimmed of the background paper, and laminated as a giant decoration affixed to her oversized pink purse. Today, I have already seen this damn flower twice and I've not even had my morning coffee. What is going on? Do they know something that I do not know? What is their draw to this flower? Was it a fun brand they advertised on the television? It was times like this that I wished that I watched television so that I was in the know.

Despite the confusion and questions, the knot in my stomach continued to loosen. Arriving at the correct building, I stop by my favorite nearby café and pick up my regular coffee before heading up to my office. As I walk through the Art Decco lobby on my way to the elevator banks, I happened to look down and see the image on every single magazine in the building's lobby. I stop walking and turn in a full circle examining every coffee table and the random magazines that have been left on the leather couches.

The same anemone flower image is on all the covers.

Was I in a dream? What is happening?

The knot in my sides was even further reduced, thinking more and more of my past...

I wonder...is this a message? Was I supposed to be doing something?

I had survived tortures no human should endure, yet I am a successful advertising executive living in a swanky, downtown loft. I don't have sex for money, I don't do drugs. I was living a life that most people envied. Oh, what little did they know about the demons I carry. Perhaps it was time for those demons to be released? What kind of life would I have if I could see things clearly for how they were, right now, today, and not how I want them to be, or how I fear they will disintegrate into? The very thought of releasing Shadow was invigorating and I enjoyed the feelings that it brought to me after so long of feeling nothing. I decided I would do what was needed to be done to release Shadow and let her go...to find closure. Hopefully I can explain to her why I had to lock her away. I just could not deal with her hurt or her rage while I was battling so much trying to get on my feet. It took longer than I expected, however, I never thought I would get here.

So, maybe I was early.

Part Two

Falling ....

Feeling the wind escape beneath my weightless body

The tickling felt between my fingers and toes

My stomach being tossed carelessly like luggage on an airline

Hair perpetually out of my eyes

A perfect opportunity to watch my descent

I fall into a pit of darkness

A vacuum of nothingness

A place where ideas are retired

No beginning and without end

Chapter Six

My palms are sweaty. I can feel the blood course through my veins just barely contained under my skin. My heart races as though I've been chased. My breathing is shallow, musty air barely enters a portion of my lungs. Shallow, quick ins and outs, not heard, not felt, but I'm alive, so I must be breathing. My head swirls in thoughts. Condemning thoughts, questions, uncertainty, doubt, fear.

I walk down a humid and darkened corridor; the walls are old and mossy, water drips from the brick at the arched hallways, tapping on the old metallic pendant lights swaying rhythmically from the deafening silence. Only my timid footsteps padding down the halls can be heard pinging off the walls in a creepy symphony with the drumming of the water droplets.

The hall twists and turns through open doorways, under chains, and through gaps in closed gates. Somehow, I feel like I've been here before. I don't feel lost. It all feels safe and familiar.

Her door is the last at the end of the corridor that I've been walking down for seemingly ever: old and wooden, with heavy, hand-forged hinges. A tiny circular window in the top/middle of the door is adorned with bars. The handle has been torn away and replaced with locks and chains. The dust on the chains and locks is so thick it looks as though the metal objects are made of fuzzy wool.

The inside is quiet.

I knock.... softly...almost as if attempting to not wake the giant. I clear my throat and realize my mouth is so dry, my voice is lost in my body. I'm so parched and am second guessing my intentions. I knock again, a little louder.

BOOOM!!!

The noise scared me out of my skin, so much so, that I jump and fell backward; flinching, anticipating what the next loud, thunderous roar.

Silence.

I open my mouth to speak but nothing comes out. A tiny crackle, shards of a voice, takes its' place instead. I cover my mouth, trying desperately to steady my breathing and heartbeat. Big deep breath in, I almost faint. My head spins from the oxygen high. My heartbeat is felt on my shirt now, beating so strongly. I uncover my mouth and try again, "Hh...h...hello?"

Silence is the response, but now I hear tiny footsteps, smaller than mine, on the other side of the door. I can hear this small person press themselves against the door...listening, quiet.

I scramble to my feet in a panic. My body wants to run, but my brain has me frozen. I take a step closer to the door and hear the person slide down to the bottom. I mimic what I hear and get on my knees. The pain on my knees is searing. I don't see wounds on my, but feel the stinging pain as though my knees are cut up or bruised.

I reach down for my strength and ask again, "Hello?" What I heard in response was curious. I heard the tiniest of voices call back in return, "Hi". It was the smallest voice I'd ever heard, sounding high pitched and unsure.

The fear rose once again in my stomach, up past my ribs, and into my chest. I begin to sweat, despite being cold. I want to run, but instead I walk in a hurried panic to the door and begin to fumble with the chains.

"Are you okay? Oh my god, I can get you out of here!"

I can hear the person push away from the door and quietly respond, "Please don't." I stop with the chains, as the dust is in a cloud everywhere from the chains being jostled, which created a tickling sensation on my nose. I begin again, pulling at each of the three locks trying to see if one was left unlocked. As I am inspecting, I call again, "Why?" I ask her, "Why should I not? Let me help you", I distractedly call out.

"Please STOP!!" a voice from behind the door booms, almost not from the same timid body that told me "hi" earlier. Startled, I stop. I raise my hands, palms to the door, and step back. I sit down in front of the door. For the first time, I am calm.

My heart seems to fill with emotion when the shuffling footsteps ring out from the other side of the door. My eyes are feeling hot, and my eyes burning, filling up with liquid...Hot fluid flows from my eyes, streaming down my cheeks in silence. *Why.... why.... why.... why.... why will she not let me help her? Why will she not help me?* I think in a mantra trance.

I snap out of it and call out, "I have to continue."

Silence.

I retake my place at the chains: inspecting, touching, lifting, twisting. The rustle of the metal and loud banging of the chains on the wooden door echoes for miles down the hall. I try and look through the window, but I can't see anything, only darkness. No windows, nothing.

How can anyone be kept here? My tears are flowing quicker now and my breathing a bit erratic as I claw into the chains and locks.

On second thought, I don't have a key...where is the key?!?

I look everywhere around the door frame. *There!* On a hook impossibly close to the door itself is an old ring of keys, dusty and webbed with spider lace. I tear the keys from their home and the feeling hits me. The darkness chills me as though an arctic blast found its way down these halls. My heart seems to have stopped beating, my breathing seems to be shallower. I freeze while I listen, holding what little breath I take in. I cannot hear the person on the other side any longer.

The fear is building.... the doom and panic are prickly on my skin. I insert a key into the first lock. Spinning the key, I can hear the metal tumblers fall and click into place. The padlock clicks open and falls to the ground in a deafening boom and clang. At this moment, a gentle breeze could be felt from the door. Curious, as there are apparently no windows or other doorways, on the other side, which would explain the sensations.

I walk my fingers around the rest of the keys, carefully selecting the next one. I touch the next lock, which feels ice cold, almost burning my fingers. I pull my hand back and make a fist to warm my cold fingers. I reach again, with determination, and re-locate the icy lock. I confidently insert the key into the padlock and hear the sleepy clicks as it falls to the floor again in a metallic thud.

The cold breeze seems colder, the silence seems thicker. There is one lock left wrapped in the chains. The lock swings gently from the breeze and from the motion of the other removed locks. I freeze and just stare. There is one unused key left on the ring. A metallic skeleton-type key with a familiar Celtic knot design on the bow. I can feel the power of the key calling to the lock. "Open me," the door seems to chant. Without thinking, I begin to rub my thumb along the Celtic knot on the key. The raised nubs on the ornate design draws up a memory from many years ago. How curious to see this design again; *I was 17 last time I saw this knot, how could I forget it?* My thumb is beginning to warm from the friction of moving my thumb back and forth on the key.

I'm transported back in time, locked in a memory...

Chapter Seven

A comforting, silent blackness holds me before a rhythmic and high-pitched beeping breaks through the stillness. A hushed chatter begins to fade into the ambient noise surrounding me. In a hazy dream darkness, an older, white man's face forms in my view. Bushy, white eyebrows seem to point to the middle of his face to his nose. Blurry and out of focus, his body seems to form from a swirling, milky haze, cloaked in a white lab-looking coat, adorned with a vibrant red Celtic knot patch stitched on the chest pocket. I notice his lips move; however, the noise that he speaks seems delayed by a few seconds. Like a dubbed movie.

"Catheter" a sleepy voice slowly calls after his face stops moving. I start to hear many voices now, but cannot make out the words: men and women all talking in unison, in muted whispers. A woman's voice returns the word, "catheter." The incessant beeping becomes softer, fading in the distance, "Blood pressure ninety over forty," a high-pitched woman's voice calls out above the chatter. The man's lips again move; his mouth stretches large and wide, and his tongue moves to his teeth, just before his lips form a circle. The voice booms in the same dubbed fashion, "We're losing her." The darkness again swallows my view of the man with the eyebrows. Ink is spilled over the pictures, everything goes black. The noise and voices fade out and only darkness remains.

The dread fills me up again as the rubbing I'm doing with my thumb on the key has made the key red hot, burning my thumb and hand, I'm snapped from my past. I look to the door, but still nothing from the other side. Just stillness. The darkness from the tiny barred window seems to be eating the door and the hallway that I am standing in. I try and calm my nerves by inhaling a big breath. While holding it, I stop rubbing the key, and exhale, finding my resolve. I swallow hard, staring at the door, trying to make sense of it all.

There are no sounds coming from the direction of the door. The breeze has turned into a wind; an icy wind, at that.

Cold and frosty, it burns my lungs as I inhale. My skin is electric from gooseflesh and my hair stands on end.

This is it.

My hand trembles as it cuts through the darkness, reaching for the last lock. I touch the lock and it again seems to freeze to my hand. There is no going back now. I follow my other trembling hand with the hot key. The key is shaking so badly now, I cannot seem to get the key into the lock. *Calm down*, I think, *One big breath in and out.* I squeeze my eyes closed and try and calm my nerves.

I press my lips together in concentration and successfully insert the key. The wind stops. An eerie calm wrap me up. I can now hear soft sobbing in the distance behind the door. A child crying, far away, in a long time past. I slowly turn the key; the clicks sound more like booms as they echo off the corridor walls. The padlock releases, but instead of letting it fall, I hold it in my hand. I try to quietly remove the padlock and put it with the keys into my pocket.

Chapter Eight

I am removing the chains and trying to be quiet, however, it's anything but quiet. Finally, all the chains have been slid off the door and thrown in a corner. With no door handle, I stand looking at the door, wondering how it might open...*push or pull?* Once the echoing stops from the chains, I take a step forward and the door seems to anticipate my movement, slowly creaking open. The darkness seems to gulp down the door. I freeze, waiting for a tiny person to emerge; however, only stillness.

Seemingly, hours have passed since I first came upon the door, even though I know it's only been a few moments. Another deep breath. I take a step closer toward the door and press one hand flatly upon it. I'm surprised at the weight of the door.

How could such a heavy door open on its own before?

I press with all my might, and it reluctantly creaks open. Darkness. I call to the abyss, "Hello?" Quiet. I take another step and cross over the threshold, into the darkness. I am swallowed wholly and can see nothing, not even my hand when I press it to my face. It's as if I've gone blind.

Though the hallway is behind me and lit, no light enters the room. The light seems to wait in the hallway, too scared to follow. I try and will the light to come in with me, but it does not. I can see nothing; I can feel nothing, but more wet, even colder air. Discouraged, I call out, "Please come out, to me... into the light."

I back up to give *something* room. What, I am not sure, but I step back anyway. I am back in the hallway, engulfed in the light. I can feel movement in the darkness, like a fog in the night. A small girl emerges.

For a second, I feel totally ridiculous. I am afraid of a girl no older than six? How funny! But then I *see* the girl. She is anything but sweet and small.   The sadness in her face strikes me first. Her denim overall dress is dirty, frayed, and stained. Her hair, golden and braided into pigtails, is draped upon her shoulders, tied with what might have been white ribbons; however, the ribbons were now yellowed and tarnished blending with her fine hair.

Her eyes were huge and sad, cheeks tear-stained and flush with red. Her hands were bloodied and busted, nails torn and broken, her knuckles mutilated and raw, and her wrists embedded with twine from when she was bound and tied. Her arms are speckled with bruises, unhealed from time. Dark and angry bruises from neglectful demons, their tight grip as they dragged her to hell. Her legs are torn apart, red from the blood.

Is the blood hers? Is it someone else's? Just raw flesh, speckled with gravel and debris, hung from her knees.

She is silent. She doesn't open her mouth; not to speak, not to cry, not to smile, or even to scream. She just stares at me with her impossibly blue eyes...longing for something...salvation...acceptance? The sight of her zaps me to another memory, a time long ago.

I squeeze my eyes shut, gulp down my fear, and let her show me...

Chapter Nine

A pounding in my temples awoke me. My heart, whilst in my slumber, has somehow relocated to my eyeballs. The pressure behind my eyes and in my ears was immense, as if I was 20,000 leagues under the sea, my skull feeling like it was going to implode. I attempt to alleviate the pain in my eyes by squeezing them tightly shut. I do so, imagining squeezing a balloon until it pops. Simultaneously, I try and push my tongue around my mouth to fully embrace waking up; however, the tongue feels cemented to the roof of my mouth. I cannot open my mouth, my lips feel as if there is only a single strip of tissue, sewn closed. "Shit, I have had some fucked up dreams, but last night's feature was supremely morbid. What the fuck did all that mean?" I think as my mind returns to my mouth. Gross, my tongue is now a prisoner of my face. I lift my arm to touch my lips, but the appendage stops moving, at what feels like only a few inches up. "What the hell?!" My eyes snap open. A bright light blinds me at first, flooding my throbbing eyes, making my head feel like it was being ripped open from every direction. A white, empty room comes into focus. It's unfamiliar, but I now notice a bleach smell in the room and a handwashing sink in the corner before a hallway. The blinds have been closed but the light in the room is just as bright as if I were on the surface of the sun. There are more lights than ceiling tiles and every single one seems to be 'on'. "Where the fuck am I?" My eyes wander to my hands then feet as I can feel sleepy panic rise in my chest. My arms and legs are adorned with thick leather bracelets with hard, shiny silver buckles on each belt. The leather straps appear to be affixed to the side of a hospital-type bed. I see a call button near my head, but the sick bastard who put me here must have realized that I could not reach the fucking button with these straps so tight. I continue to survey my strange environment. My head pounds each time my heart beats. Despite the pain behind my eyes, I keep looking for clues. There are several machines surrounding me. One machine that is full of blinking lights, rigid waves being drawn across a black screen. The machine beeps and flashes a small, white heart. A second machine has two bags of clear liquid above them; they seem to be dispensing fluid every few beeps, from the bag above, down the tubes lead into my arm. A third machine appears to be holding a yellow bag at the foot of my bed. I have stickers with cords attached all over my chest and stomach, the cables are coming out of blankets attached to yet another machine that seems to be printing endless amounts of paper, lines drawn up and down in no sort of pattern at all. I notice as my body begins to awake, my fingers and toes are numb from either being cold or from the sheer tautness of the straps. My fingertips are devoid of color and the pale tips contrast the rest of my body. The machine beeps and the throbbing percussion in my eyes seem to be making horrible music together. I am so tired, I want to panic more; however, I feel barely able to move and my mouth is so devoid of moisture I can't scream. As I lay, helpless, I think of wild scenarios as to how I could have found myself here, just as I hear a loud click down the hallway of my room. The door hesitantly swings open, slowly revealing an almost black and white, heavy set nurse with dark hair and old, tired eyes. Her face catches my open eyes and she turns from black and white to a vibrant color as her mouth stretches to a grotesque smile revealing crooked and yellowed teeth.

"Oh! You're awake!" she calls in almost a sing-song voice.

Her perkiness pisses me off. "How can she be so bright and cheery, while I'm strapped to a fucking bed with a crushing headache and numb fingers and toes?" Somehow, despite my mouth being gone from my face, I manage to snap, "Bitch, if you were doing your fucking job, I would be able to feel my hands and feet. Where the hell am I?" I croak.

Ignoring my hate, she gives an even bigger smile and says, "You were intubated, Honey. Your throat's gonna be sore for a little while. I'll get ya some ice chips."

Ignoring her last clue, I again bark, "Where the fuck am I?"

Her smile recedes slightly, "You're at St. Luke' hon. The third floo..."

"Who the fuck cares what floor I'm on, how did I get here?" I interrupt.

Her face turns from cheery to more serious and her gaze shifts to the fluid bags above my head. As if on command, she busies her hands, "Well, it's no wonder I did not recognize you. Must be your first time. Poor thing. I don't know the details, but originally, you were brought in by ambulance for an attempted suicide. Got close too! Thank god your neighbor found you and called 9-1-1. The third floor is the mental wellness ward."

"Suicide? I never tried to kill myself last night, I was at home."

The nurse seemed to chuckle, but it sounded more like a snort, "Last night?" The nurse repeated while still chucking, she turned to look at me. Her smile faded completely as she saw confusion splashed across my face. Somberly, she adds, "Oh…Honey, you came in three weeks ago."

No one spoke again while she was in the room. She began to unbuckle the straps as I zoned out, traveling beyond the pounding eyes, and back to 'three weeks'. Her voice seemed to echo in my mind. That did not make sense. 'Three weeks'. Again, her echo. I was just at home, doing math homework. That was not three weeks ago…that was last night. I just had a weird dream, that's all. This isn't real. 'Three weeks'. She echoed again. I remember the math homework so vividly. Algebra, solve for x…Attempted suicide? Have I been asleep this whole time, what is happening? I watched the nurse remove the IV needle from my arm. 'Three weeks'. Her voice bounced again off the walls of my brain. Was the weird dream, not a dream at all? The nurse silently wrapped my arm tightly where the IV was. I was snapped out of my mantra-like state when she removed the catheter. The nurse left briefly before returning with ice chips, water, and pills. I don't remember telling her my head was hurting, but I was grateful for the pills and ice chips. As I lift the pills to my mouth, I notice my wrists, a muddied wash of purples, greens, and blues swirled in a mix of earthy tones in the shape of the wide bracelets, welcoming your eyes to my still white fingertips. Later that day, I was being transferred to the inpatient ward of the third floor.

Part Three

Into the darkness I fall

The mouth of the beast swallows me up

The belly is soft and cold

As I lay, I wonder if my eyes are still open

'Who is the beast', I ask

I await to be digested wholly

The deafness in the belly cushions my head

Swirling in memories like bisque in a blender

Dizzy and dazed I lay dreaming

Waiting for calm, hoping for peace

Peace is why I fell

Love and the pursuit of freedom are why I stay

Chapter Ten

I gasp for air as if I've been under water. I wildly blink tears away, as my eyes dart around the room trying to remember where and in what time I am in. I fight the memories.

She's doing something to me.

Somehow, the sight of her releases a flood of days past. An incoming barrage of memories floods in my mind, despite the sandbags placed years ago to keep them out.

I don't want to remember, I don't want to be here.

I try to not look at her small frame and dirty face. I avoid her sky-blue eyes, though I can feel them burning holes into me. The memories don't stop coming despite me averting my eyes from her. I cannot stand to look away from her much longer, my eyes are being lured to her. The memories are feeling more intense. My eyes snap back to her small broken body standing in front of the blackness that is her open door. Magnets locking my eyes on her. I do nothing but stare. I'm frozen, yet the panic begins to take me over. I examine her wounds, her beautiful and soft features. Her eyes command attention to her face. Her eyes seem to escort me down into the mouth of madness. I cannot fight the memories back much longer. She is far stronger than I am. She blinks her huge eyes slowly as if under water, while raising one eyebrow as if to say, "Let's go...." *I'm so afraid.* I spent decades trying to forget, but I guess I knew what I had set out to do down here. I should have known there would be a price and if it was not my life, then it was a nominal price to pay. Peace rarely came free and it almost never came without struggle. So, here I am, in front of her, imagining what she must think of me. I bet she thinks I'm weak or worse yet, a coward. How could she not think ill of me? After all, it was me that trapped her down here. I begin to lose control of my mind, which is what she wanted all along. She wanted me to give her the control that she never had. Shadow had always been the one being controlled. The one forced to act for the men, the clients. No one ever trusted her to survive. They just took and took and expected her to live and endure. They convinced her that her only job was to be someone else's pleasure, never her own.

That realization ushered in the memories, bombarding me with rapid images blinking, one by one of faces I'd met, places I'd traveled, things I'd done; people and things I'd spent a lot of energy in blocking out. Ticking down, scene by scene again in 1998, blinking, fixated on age 17. More and more images of that time soak through my tightly wrapped mind like an oozing wound through a bandage. I moved out of my parents' house just two years prior. I remain in that time, flooded with the memories of the second overdose, the dumb cat puzzle, the looney bin...

I remember everything as if I'm reliving the time...

Chapter Eleven

I'm wheeled from the ICU to a private room behind locked double doors. The room was a plain square shape, with a stubby hallway to the main door. The very uncomfortable looking hospital bed was along the back wall, there was a small chair in the middle the room that did not seem to belong, and a moveable table next to the chair. To almost rub in that you were alone, there was not even a second chair for a guest to sit in. Unless I would be strapped to a bed, and then the guest would get the funny blue chair. "I already hate it here," I think as I rotate my right, ugly, blue-green restraint-bruised wrist in my left hand clockwise, and then counterclockwise. The bruises were fresh and left an obvious line where the leather straps dug into my wrists and ankles. "I wonder how long I was in restraints," I mumble to myself. There is a private bathroom in the hallway and a blue, metallic school locker before the door to the bathroom. A pointless feature in my room, as I have no belongings here, no idea if anyone even knows I'm here. I have (or had) an apartment, but I was given five days to pay rent the day I was doing homework. That was three weeks ago, apparently. Surely, I was homeless by now. It was an obvious hospital room, devoid of any warmness or comfort. The nurse in the ICU ward explained to me that I came in naked by ambulance, so I am stuck in this pastel pink gown and an old pair of grey sweatpants that had been left years ago by a nameless lost soul. There, on the uncomfortable bed was a schedule of "mandatory" activities that I was forced to choose from; "it was like summer camp for the insane. The schedule is ridiculous. And I'm fucking depressed; forcing me to put together kitty puzzles with fucked up bitches would only increase my desire to do whatever the fuck I did to land my ass in here in the first place." I sit, think on the corner of the bed, reviewing the ridiculous schedule, glance at my wrists, back-and-forth between the two. The bruises were pretty bracelets that seemed to bring out my eyes. The crazy parts. Because of the colored bands, the effect made it appear that I was wearing white gloves and white socks. The tie-dyed appendages really seemed to say all the wrong things. Nothing says crazy like restraint bruises. After I was shown my room, I was given a few minutes to remind myself that I have nothing to put in the blue locker. I'm corralled into a dusty, pink floral wallpapered waiting room with plastic chairs along one wall, and a floral print loveseat in the middle of the room, situated on an ill-matching rug that points to a huge wooden television. It's a very old television that comes encased in a wooden, waist-high entertainment bench that fills the entire back wall of the rectangular room. The top appears to lift, possibly revealing an old turntable. The television was color, but the colors were monotone and faded. Just as predicted, there is a card table, opposite of the plastic chairs, with a partially put together kitten puzzle. The dusty box on the table appears to have been there in that same position for years. The pieces have been put together all along the border, but the middle was left open. All along the edges of the partially-assembled puzzle, the pieces were chaotic. They appeared to be pieces for three different puzzles. An ocean of blues, yellows, pinks, and whites and cardboard all Pollocked on every exposed part of that table. There are two youngish girls on the couch. They sat motionless, staring at the TV, or at least in the direction of the TV. I proceeded to sit in one of the plastic chairs and folded my arms in protest. The Nutty Professor was on the television, looking mostly black and white. The sound was so low I could not hear anyone speak.

"Code Blue" I heard a deadpan nurse call from in front of me.

The same monotone nurse badges the doors and they click open, birthing two police officers, each holding the arm of a woman. I can't bear to look at her.

"Fuck off me" She yells. "Eat shit, Bastard Pig!" she screams again.

"Yeah, yeah." One of the officers seems to read from a script memorized in his mind, "You're safe now." He says monotone.

Both officers seemed unfazed by this whole circus. It occurs to me that I have no idea what day it is. I ask one of the motionless girls on the couch, "What day is it?"

Neither girl stirs in response.

I roll my eyes and yell, "What fucking day is it??"

Somehow the woman is already long gone and only the officers and the head nurse are left between the doors and the nurses' station. They all stop their conversation to look at me. One of the officers says something but I cannot hear, and they all laugh in response as they stare at me. The head nurse walks to the doors and taps her badge to the wall, making the hinged apparatuses click open as the officers exited. Afterwards, the nurse walks to my chair and smiles a smile as fake as the flowers on the faded wallpaper.

"I bet Sarah," she nods to one of the girls on the couch, "would like to help put together the puzzle." Her head then rolls slowly over shoulder to the puzzle along the wall. The girl does not even blink, she may not have blinked since I've been in here. Christ, is she even real? I get up from my chair. The nurse seems energized that for the first time, that someone is doing what she suggested. But I didn't, I walked to the girl that I thought was Sarah and I stood towering over her, just staring. Waiting for a twitch or a blink. Nothing. I raise my finger and jab it into the side of the girl's face; her jaw relaxes and her cheek caves through. leading me past her teeth and into her mouth. The nurse's mouth drops open as she stares at me. I begin to withdraw my finger as if I knew that was how Sarah needed to be booted up.

She jerks a bit and blurts out sleepily, "What?"

I said, "You Sarah?"

"Uh...um, yeaah."

"Fuck it," I think. I go back to my room, as the nurse was calling behind me to keep my hands to myself.

Chapter Twelve

It's been two weeks since I've been at Camp Crazy. My restraint bruises are all but yellow bands now. Every day, I've had to choose from a list of activities to fill the time. An asinine list of items that really drive home that you've become insane: crafts, group therapy, workshops for practicing how to be a 'normie' for when you get out…I'd managed to skip a few days at first, but they caught on quickly. I did, however, manage to avoid any kind of personal relationship with every other guest on the third floor. I did not small talk, and in group, I agreed with every other girl and her pedantic personal revelation. Crafts are my favorite. I've tried to just hang out doing crafts all day, but they really see no value in art, sadly. To date, I've been contained within this hospital for five weeks, and not a soul has visited, called, or inquired about my whereabouts.

Though I had no one come calling, and I called no one, I secretly wanted my mother. We had not spoken since I moved out. She said I was too young to move out on my own. Of course, I was too young! I was only 15 years old, but the alternative, staying there…I couldn't do that either. Fuck her to even ask that of me. I had been lucky, and since I had always been a planner, I had an apartment all lined up. I had saved all my cash from jobs and clients for months, and I found a back-alley landlord that would rent, off the books, to a kid that paid in cash. I found a normal job at the mall in a department store. Luckily, they did not ask for a work permit. It did not pay great, but it was enough to pay the rent and have some money left over for food. The one-bedroom apartment itself was not fancy. There was carpet and a small kitchen, but it was a typical basement: musty, dark, and full of strange bugs. All that aside, it was impressive for a kid to come up with on her own. Despite being okay for a couple of years, the fact that I still wanted a mother remained, someone that I could ask questions to. My body is changing, my world has changed. I wanted a mother to help make sense of it all. However, I did not have that that luxury. Our relationship was strained, we argued a lot. I spat at her and called her names. I pushed her away. I feel uncontrollable rage when I see her, and I cannot hide my resentment toward her for how she just gave me to her parents to raise. I felt the sting of abandonment all these years later. I'm only seventeen, for Christ's sake. A seventeen-year-old that has been alone in the hospital for over a month, scared. I think about her often.

"I wonder if she thinks of me."

It was not long before the doctors decided it would be a good idea to start tests on the abandoned girl suffering from life. I did not talk much, nor tell them why I was so sad. I could not talk about things that happened at home. That was the first rule. And besides, I was not there anymore, no need to talk about it. I just wanted either peace or death. So instead of talking, they ran tests to find out what was going on inside that head of mine. They glued wires to my skull, my chest while asking me to look at pictures, listen to talking, or answer yes or no questions. They put me through tight tubes and had me lie perfectly still for hours while the machine knocked and banged in an almost Morse code. They put me through a giant suspended donut that seemed to contain a tiny galaxy. The donut hummed and lights blinked all around my head. The infinite matrix of glowing lights and blinking colors mesmerized me. Doctors came in asking ridiculous questions regarding if I heard voices that were not present. "I wasn't crazy, I was being sold to various people in town," I thought. But I went along with their games. I told them that I did hear voices. Truth be told, I knew that they were memories, but I would not mind something to block them out. I can still feel their touches, their smell lingers in my nostrils, and on my body despite being away from that for years. I left those parts out though. Better to not give them too much information. The memories of the voices were horrible, though. Screaming obscenities at me, reminding me that I am worthless and good for one thing only. I get queasy every time I think about those times, and so I force away the memories, choking down the rage. After the tests came back, the doctors thought it best to medicate me, perhaps to keep me from realizing that I was alone in this terrible world. I began to take a salad of brightly colored pills in hues of yellows, blues, greens, and pinks. The pills made me complacent, but they also dulled the whispers and the screams. So, I take the good with the bad. The pills made me feel like I was only watching the world go by from a window. I was not actually in control to participate. The start of the third week, only a few days into the daily diet of pills, and I was no longer anything. I was not happy, not mad, not sad, not resentful... nothing. This was also about the time that I had my very first visitors, ever.

Chapter Thirteen

Murray, the deputy sheriff, and Anne, the deacon of the church, strolled into my room. Anne was holding a chocolate brown, velvet bunny with beautiful honey-colored glass eyes. The bunny has bright, bubble gum pink, silk-lined ears. The stuffed animal was as divine to look at as it had to be when held. The stitching was so fine and straight and perfect. Anne reached the bunny out to me, yet it was still just out of reach.

Simultaneously, Murray said, "Get dressed, Baby Girl. Hurry, hurry and we'll get some ice cream," in his familiar mild southern drawl. His voice made my stomach hurt but it was so familiar and oddly comforting. That was the sound of home. My stomach twisted and knotted as I tracked the bunny with my eyes, smiling indiscriminately. Without question, I hopped up and quickly walked to the blue locker in the hallway. I removed the pink gown and took down my sweatpants. Opening the noisy metallic door, I reached in and grabbed my one pair of newly donated jeans and my one donated, faded Cancun t-shirt. I was never given shoes, so I kept on the hospital brown booties. Once dressed, I was rewarded by receiving the bunny to hold. It was the softest bunny I had ever held, and it was magical. It was as if I'd been waiting for the bunny my whole life, and now my life was complete. I inspected the soft bunny, admiring the stitching and the perfectly twisted whiskers; feeling the smooth, slick ears, and snuggling my face into the bunny, smelling the sweet smell. Anne and Murray led me, with big confident smiles, out of the room and into the hall. The hall seemed to be lit just for us. We were marching in our own parade. I was going home, finally. My stomach turned and tossed and the need to throw up was intense. I coughed away some gagging. They loved me, and if I had to work to help them, then that was my duty. I coughed again at the bitter bile taste that had painted my tongue. My chest burned with hot burps. The doors somehow just swung open and we walked four magical steps toward freedom.

"Stop them!!" A familiar female voice shouted from behind us. One nurse approached, flanked by two uniformed officers that

took ahold of Anne and Murray as the nurse took me by my arm in one hand, placing her other hand on my back, turning me around and walking back toward the locked double doors, in the process of gingerly escorting me back to my room. As I walked back through the locked doors to the ward, I thought I saw my mother, in a dark corner, but no one ever came to visit again. I'm confused and upset; I mean, as upset as I can be while being medicated. I keep asking what is happening and why am I not leaving with my grandparents. The nurse explains nothing other than it is not yet time to go.

Chapter Fourteen

Anne and Murray's visit set me back another week. It's now been four weeks since I woke up strapped to the bed. I've adjusted a bit to the meds, but I am still numb to most things. I can no longer hear the voices and I can no longer feel their touches. I still feel the shame though. I think perhaps that will never depart. The disgust and anger cut me deep, despite the cocktail of pharmaceuticals. Somehow, I am going to have deal with these feelings if I am going to make it on the outside. The week dragged on and I decided that I was going to give life a chance. Why the hell not? I had attempted suicide many times and I'm still fucking here. So, might as well try another way. Maybe the meds were working.

I had been holed up for almost two months never really finding out what happened that night, seven weeks ago. I got bits and pieces from the casual, well-planted questions during group or doctor visits to discuss medication levels. I got a few juicy details from a night nurse that explained that they did not want to trigger me with details that I had been successful. She recalled what she knew; I'd somehow managed to swallow 1,800 mg of Xanax as well as other pills found in my apartment. Thing was, by the time the neighbor called 9-1-1, the drugs had already been processed by my liver and could not be neutralized or pumped out. By the time the ambulance had arrived, I was collapsed, and my heart had slowed so much that it finally gave way while en route to the hospital. They restarted my heart twice with manual compressions. Once in the ER, they restarted again using the paddles. Doctors feared brain damage from the times that I lost a heartbeat. No one knows when I took the pills or even why. Last thing I remember was doing math homework. I was, I guess, in a coma for two weeks and six days. The nurse concludes her story with, "You shouldn't be alive. That much Xanax with how little you are, combined with the other pills you took... You are a miracle."

The word, miracle made me laugh out loud.

She stops what she is doing, turns, and give me a serious look, "Nothing funny about that."

That is where we disagreed. She called it a miracle, I called it a nuisance. An annoying interruption. I had wanted to die. I don't remember taking the pills, it's true, but I had fantasized doing it all the time and attempted three times now. When I was twelve, I overdosed on Tylenol, taking 240 tablets. Before I moved out, I slit my wrists. It was not a shocker that I wanted to die. I'd just never been successful previously. It was exhilarating to know that I won that fight, the war was still raging, but I got a point nonetheless.

Chapter Fifteen

I was being discharged in the morning. I didn't have an apartment to go to anymore. Despite being evicted, my cold-ass mother managed to dig through all my shit that the landlord threw to the curb, only to pick out a journal that I sometimes wrote in. When she came to the hospital, she was so proud of herself when she handed me the old book. "Of all the dumbass things to keep, that is what you choose to dig out?" I rolled my eyes as I spoke. She came to the hospital for discharge. I don't know how she knew to come, I did not phone her. No one asked me if I knew of someone to call. She just showed up, as if it had been prearranged the whole time. She lied to the doctors, telling them that she was so happy to have her baby back and she could not wait to get her home again. She and I both knew that was all a lie.

After I climbed into her car, she said, "Well....where are you going?"

I kept my eyes forward and I told her to take me to my favorite park. We arrived at the park on the east side of town. I thanked her for the ride and as I climbed out of the car with my dumb journal, she called out, "Wait!"

I saw her walk to the trunk and pull out an old backpack and a tattered hot pink sleeping bag. She stuffed the sleeping bag into the bag and took out an old parka and stuffed that into the pack as well. She handed it to me and smiled. I did not want shit from her, but I had nothing but the clothes on my back. So I reluctantly took the backpack and that was the last time I ever saw her.

I was homeless for a few years after that. I guess I could have gone home, but the fear and shame kept me away. Three years on the street changes a kid.

It was during this time that I decided I needed to push down my rage and my pain. I had to lock her up, Shadow had to go, if I were to survive. I had to put away my darkness until there was more light. It would be the only way. My Shadow was with me always and up until this point, she had run the show.

And my life was in shambles. Getting out was her doing, for sure. I'm grateful to her as I would not have had the courage to escape on my own. I needed Shadow to take control then to live, but now I needed something different than just survival. Something that Shadow could not help with. Shadow was integral to escape, but she also seemed like she wanted to escape more than just abuse. It seemed she was the darkness calling for my escape from life altogether. I needed to know that I could survive on my own, without my shadow, in order to quell the hurt, the rage, the pain that I endured every day. The weight of what I was running from pulled me deeper and deeper into darkness. The weight of the despair seemed to slurp at my heels at every step that I took. Right now, in this moment, I had to choose. Life or death...Her or me... Shadow or light? So, I lured her down an incredible corridor, promised her peace and revenge and whatever else I could think of that she would fall for. I shoved her tiny body into the room and locked the door with three locks and three chains. I have no intention in returning, more because I don't think I will survive without her, but I must try.

Leaving the memory, I come back with guilt and shame. I've come back, and I have her in front of me now, all these years later. My cheeks and ears blush, and the feeling of defensiveness spreads through my chest and into to my arms and legs. I tense up and bristle from what I'd done.

Let her think I'm weak, I ponder.

Besides who locked who down here?

The corners of my mouth curl into a sickly smile.

I notice her still looking at me. Her blue eyes flicker, and like lasers, cut deeply into my soul. The defensiveness fades and is replaced with guilt and sorrow. I can feel my face soften; however, her face remains unchanged, statuesque, as she bores holes into me.

Chapter Sixteen

Time seems to be frozen. My mind races for something to say to break the ice. I stutter as I search for words to put into some sort of order...

"Wh, wh...why did you not want me to let you out?" I wrestle with, as if that was the wrong question to ask. I almost hold my breath in anticipation for a response; however, one does not come.

She seems to scan every inch of me, silently. She's just a child...such a small, innocent child. I kneel to her eye level and reach my arms out to embrace a hug. Her eyes track me down to her level and her head cocks slightly to the right in a robotic twitch. Her head pops back up straight and her mouth relaxes and opens as if she is about to speak.

Locusts and moths burst from her mouth in biblical proportions, a swirling black cloud of buzzing and wings. With the insects, come moans and screams and sounds, originating from nowhere else but the belly of hell. My ears seem to burst from the bellowing sound echoing, a steam engine screaming down this hallway. My ears burn and feel as if they are oozing blood from the assault of noise. My hands attempt to cover and shield my burning ears; however, the act is in vein.

I collapse into a ball on the ground, and I lie there gripping my ears and temples in pain, trying to protect my head from exploding as a result of the noise. When she finally closes her mouth, the insects have flown away, except for a few straggling moths and flies. My hearing has been replaced with a high-pitched scream in deafness.

I slowly stand, but am disoriented and weak. So cold. I realize, it's just me and her down here, miles away from anyone that could help. Alone in nothingness. The panic returns, filling my glass full. I pull my hands down from my head and ears. My eyes burn from the tears. Hot, fat tears thickly roll down my cheeks. My head falls, *what is there to do now*? I think. Surely, she wants me dead.

I guess I deserve this. I am waiting for her to kill me.

I wait for a long while before realizing she may not kill me. But what does she want? What would I want? Shadow had always wanted to absorb the hurt from others. I had always assumed that Shadow was punishing herself, like all of the suffering she endured, for someone else's benefit. But perhaps she was not trying to punish at all. Perhaps she was trying to heal. If I were Shadow, I would want to absorb my hurt and fear and tell me it will be okay. I think perhaps she absorbs hurt to try and take it from them. She is strong, perhaps stronger than anyone, and she is the only one that can endure. Perhaps, it's the amount of healing that is needed and not getting done that fuels her rage.

I reach my hand toward her slowly. I won't look at her, I can't. I stand, silently sobbing, when I feel tiny, wet fingers fill my hand. Instinctively, my fingers gently fold around her miniature hand. I am shocked, but try and remain calm. Without a word, I begin walking with her out of the hallway.

I think back to how just a couple of days earlier, I was in my apartment, confused and assaulted by unwelcomed flashbacks of fear and doom...feeling lost and alone. However, not really feeling much else. Feeling incomplete and missing a part of me. Things felt different now: the loneliness was gone, the knot in my stomach seemed to loosen. Maybe the knot would never fully leave, but if it could not be so tight, it would free me to take in cleansing breaths from time to time, and that would be a huge improvement. Truth is, I have no plan, no idea what will happen once we are out, but I imagine we will find out. Together.

Part Four

The cold Adonis Blue stretches her body

Warming her translucent wings with the rays of the sun

Ushering out the shutter of cold from the life that was before

No longer earth bound

Soon she would take to the sky

To prepare, she fans her lacey wings-

Pumping blood from her tongue to her still forming tiles

Dreaming of dancing on the wind

Chapter Seventeen

Tightly, yet gently, I held her hand and we walked slowly toward the mouth of the hallway. As we walk, I remember the knot in my stomach; the anxiety, the hurt, the crushing loneliness. I remember that feeling of being lost or having lost something...A part of me, the feelings were fading. The hurt was slipping away, just as we were slipping and slinking through widely chained gates and unlocked doors, winding around corners and on forever. No words were spoken, just the tapping water beads which provided a percussion-like beat as we walked. I slipped with ease, but even with how badly damaged her body was, the way she navigated the obstacles looked somehow graceful. Her tiny feet seemed to dance over the floor and under gates, silently. It occurs to me that the reason I've felt so broken is a literal piece of me has been locked away. Hidden from the world, apart from her whole self.

My head swirled with unanswered questions. I could feel the panic and dread, waiting on standby to fill me up again. All I could do now was walk forward. There was no going back. I could feel her tiny, wet hand in my own. Sticky from the dried blood and sharp from the hanging, busted nails. Her cold hand was velvet in my own. Despite being damaged and broken, she was still, oddly calm for being locked in a tiny, windowless room for twenty years. I squeezed her hand to let her know it was safe now, but I had no confidence in that message, and she knew it. The truth is, I have no idea what it feels like to be whole anymore. It has been so long without her, my future with her is unknown. Can life be good? Am I ready? I think of all that we endured together. I think of what I endured without her and what she endured without me. The guilt that I was feeling earlier seemed to also relax, as if all of that no longer mattered. Now think of all we can accomplish together. Think of what we can do united in our own unique strength.

We were about halfway and I could see the exit doors. Despite the newly forming hope, the dread and doom still assume their positions inside my chest. I struggled with something encouraging to say but nothing comes to mind. We finally reach the exit. Instead of ripping the doors open to the outside, I stop and stare at the doors. She stops too and I feel her looking at me, I can feel her questioning why we are not leaving, yet she does not seem anxious. More so curious. Though the tension closes in around me, and along with it, the anxiety, and the fear, I am oddly calm.

I don't know what's going to happen. I don't want to say it, but I'm afraid she'll kill squirrels and torture kittens. Should I give a speech about things and expectations? No. She is not MY child, I have no duty to her, just release her. I want to let her free and maybe then I can be free, too. Finally, the doom breaks and laps away, and fades enough for me to take a determined step toward the final doors. She does not follow; my arm is pulled back to where she remains standing.

I cock my head with confusion... I say loudly through a clenched jaw, "If you didn't want out of that room, why did you come with me? Now you won't leave?? You have to leave! What are you going to do, go back to that cell? You don't have to, you're free now!"

I am so confused. Still she does not speak. She only stares at me with that dirty face and the streaked wet cheeks. My fear has been eaten by frustration now and my eyes get hot. The hope is slipping away while my head pounds, and my cheeks turn a dark red and I turn to bark, "LETS GO!!" The echo seems to shout over and over and I am frightened by my own booms, instantly embarrassed at my outburst. I fear that I may have scared her, but when I finally sheepishly look at her, she is grinning at me. She seems to have been entertained by my brief rage. Yet, she stands there unmoving, unspeaking. Silently staring. I pull at her harder now, and though she is a small six-year-old, she is firmly cemented to the ground. I cannot lift her, push, or pull her. She is made of heavy rock and I am only a mere mortal, incapable of moving a child. I am trying many things, bribery even...though I'm not surprised that didn't work this time.

Finally, I feel out of options and kneel again....my ears just got the hearing back and I fear she will deafen me again, but I hope to understand, and I'll hope she'll speak to help me. God knows I have a ton to explain to her... somehow. I don't know how I'll do that if she does not open up to talk to me.

Chapter Eighteen

I look at her sweet, sad face. I examine her more closely now; I remember all her wounds. I remember the dentist tying the rope around *my* wrists to keep me from fighting him off; my wrists begin to ache. I remember the sheriff shoving me to my knees every weekend, into the gravel after dragging me out of the car. The gravel tore my legs apart into scraps and removed chunks of flesh from my legs. I remember screaming for him to leave me be, just for one night; I also remember him backhanding *me* in response. My jaw throbs. I remember the blood, so much blood. I remember the superintendent of the school beating me over and over before ripping off my He-Man Undaroos. I feel my stomach turn and bubble. I remember the pastor's wife scrubbing my body in bleach and scolding hot water to wash *my* sins away, while my grandmother, the deacon, watched from the doorway. The tears have found their way back out of my eyes and I begin to tremble with memories. I squeeze my eyes shut, as if to block them out. The remembering has always made me sad… but now I can also feel *her*. I feel the rage, the anger for what we endured. I feel the hate that rolls and bubbles in my belly, low and deep. Tears roll freely down my cheeks and my breathing is shallow and erratic. I remember when they came to our school to talk about abuse. My breathing becomes more erratic and I breathe in bursts as I remember raising my hand to tell the adults about how my grandfather makes feel bad from touching. I remember how small they made me feel, reminding me that my grandfather was the deputy in the town, and everyone knew how much he loved me. Everyone's face so somber staring at me in disgust for me to say something. "How dare you?," their eyes seemed to chant. I remember, that was the last time I told anyone. The tears fell freely now, spilling down my cheeks, mirroring Shadow's ivory streaked face. I can feel the rage building, slowly edging out the fear, and the defeat.

"Dammit!! Let's get fucking out of here!!" I scream at her.

Unflinching, she stays put. Her mouth seems fixed in a dark smile.

Wiping away my tears, I look her in the eyes and shout, "Fine!! You won't leave, I won't make you." I turn away from her, toward the door. I walk to the door and put my hands on the cool handles. I pause. I can't leave her down here... again.... My head hangs but I swing the doors open anyway and immediately the sun drenches me and blinds me from the bright. I turn back to her to look at her, hopefully get her to come with me; however, she is not there. I am alone. I wildly turn around and look down the hallway. Surely, she did not...she could not have run back to the room in just the two seconds it took me to open the doors?

I can't leave her down here,

I think over and over. I let go of the doors and the sound of them shutting seems so permanent. Though I've let her out of the locked room, the guilt of leaving her in this hallway is too much, so I wildly begin running back down the hallway toward her door. I look in corners, around doors and gates, over debris. Where could she have gone? There is nothing. Only stillness. I reach her door and the door is still wide open. I go in and see with my fingers, touching every brick that lines the black room, every inch in the darkness. Nothing, no one. I am so confused, I walk to the doors, alone. Despite her not being here, I can still feel her. I can feel her rage, her power. I lift my hand to my face, and I can see the blood left from when she gave me her hand to hold. I know she was here...wasn't she? I walk back down the winding corridor. Finally, I reach the doors again, and push them open slowly; half-expecting her to be behind me, I turn once more to look. I am still alone.

Chapter Nineteen

Somehow, I knew, she would be gone. I am not sad, because I know she is not gone at all. She is right back where she belongs, inside of me. Shadow and I are one again. I can feel her innocence, her power. I sense her fear of the future, yet her confidence in her ability to succeed. I can feel her rage, but I feel the compassion that she brings. She is a force. I am a force. The rage seems to balance the fear. Neither are gone or more than before, but somehow, I am more at peace. I feel more balanced. I don't know what the future looks like any more than she can or even if it will be a good one. I know my chances of finding some kind of meaning from all of this are greater with Shadow, guiding me. Shadow was strong. She was a survivor; I had always viewed her as the strong one. I had felt like I was what was left over after a war. A "used-to-be" person, with an area for hopes and dreams that would be inserted when they were thought of, but no thoughts ever came, no dreams formed. I never expected to live without Shadow, so I never tried, and clearly, I did not. I had only been going through the motions of life, pursuing what I thought one should pursue. There was no soul or heart in anything that I did. I took a deep breath, and decided I was ready for the next steps to the rest of my life.

The sun is a golden yellow and it blankets everything in its warmth. I take my first step out of the damp hallway, into the warmth of the sun. The sun seemed to move with me; however, my mind is so busy with racing thoughts, questions, and doubts that I don't notice. I take a second step; the ground begins to shake, trembling under my feet. Mentally, I am replaying the recent events over and over in my head and seem to not feel the earth below my feet. I begin walking more steadily now, just walking, unknown of a destination, I just walk. The sun lights my path in front of me, but all I notice is how the light is hot and the light seems more intense than I have ever felt before. The sunlight seems to have blocked out the pale, cloudless sky and continues to grow more intense.

The light and heat change distract me from the day's events, and so while walking, I look up. The sun is so close that I can feel the solar flares licking my forehead. Each step I take, I can feel the immense heat on me, cooking me. My hair is blown back from the hot air blowing against my face. I also notice the earth shaking under my footsteps. In the distance, all around me, I can hear tiny rocks falling and the dirt cascading down mountains and mesas from my earth-shaking steps.

I stop walking and the earth's trembling has also subsided. The rocks continue to cascade down the mountains, but new rocks do not fall without my footsteps. The sun is still burning my face; shielding the rays from my face with my hand, I curse the heat aloud, "Damn this sun!"

Immediately, the sun is blanketed in dark grey clouds. The hot is snubbed out and replaced by soft, fat, fluffy bellies full of rain. I hadn't noticed clouds in the sky earlier today, but I am grateful for the break in the UV rays. And after all, I do love the rain.

I feel different, yes, now I can really feel it. The energy, the life have both returned to my cold body, warming and re-energizing me. The addition of Shadow has filled me up like a match drenches a dark room in light. It seemed to fan lit shadow's embers, and breathe life back into her. As a result, her cold, barely glowing coals broke into a hot flame that it seemed to bring life back to my world.

I don't feel lost. I know exactly where I am going. I look to the grey sky; the clouds part and the wind whispers, "Onward, child. It's time to go…"

The End…?

About The Author

Dharma, while searching for her path, enjoys making art. She's a Buddhist by destiny, on a journey into her own mind, and the minds of others, on her quest to understand her own inner demons, angels, heroes, and villains. Sequestered peacefully on the western slope, Dharma regularly puts out an independent magazine promoting personal freedom. Dharma believes the only way to truly own one's life is to become aware of one's surroundings; as well as, be fully independent from the state.